TEN TERRIBLE DINOSAURS

Paul Stickland

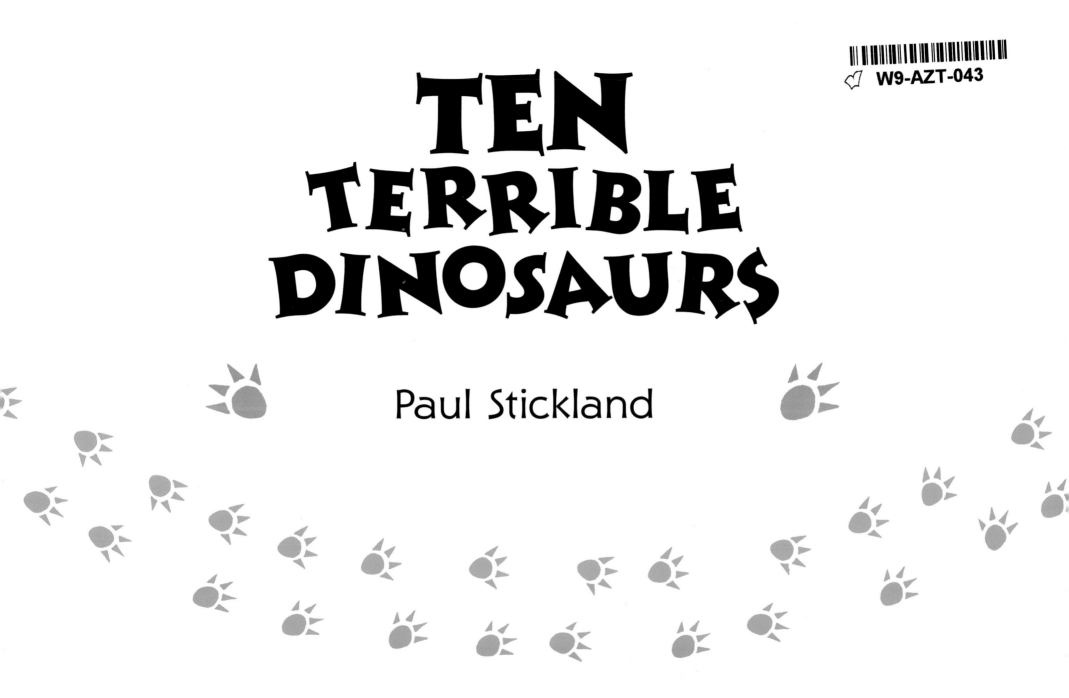

DUTTON CHILDREN'S BOOKS · NEW YORK

10 terrible dinosaurs

standing in a line

soon began to push and shove

until there were...

9 enormous dinosaurs

—their dancing was just great,

but one was much too spiky,

so then there were...

8 elated dinosaurs who

thought they were in heaven,

but one nearly popped,

so then there were...

7 silly dinosaurs,

playing goofy tricks,

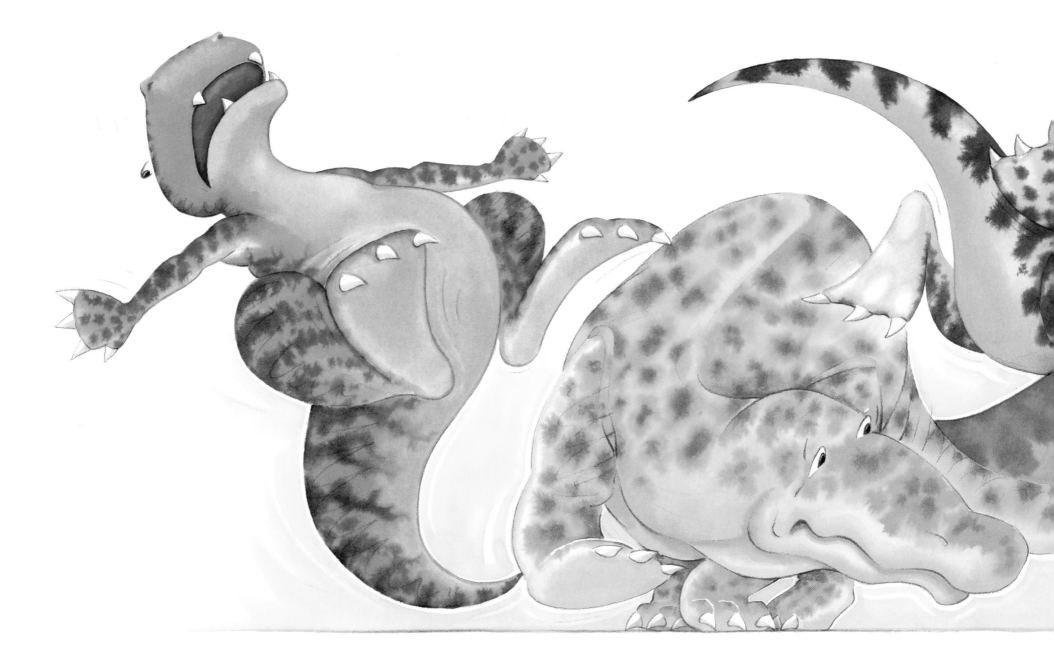

but one went too far,

so then there were...

6 stomping dinosaurs

who danced a crazy jive,

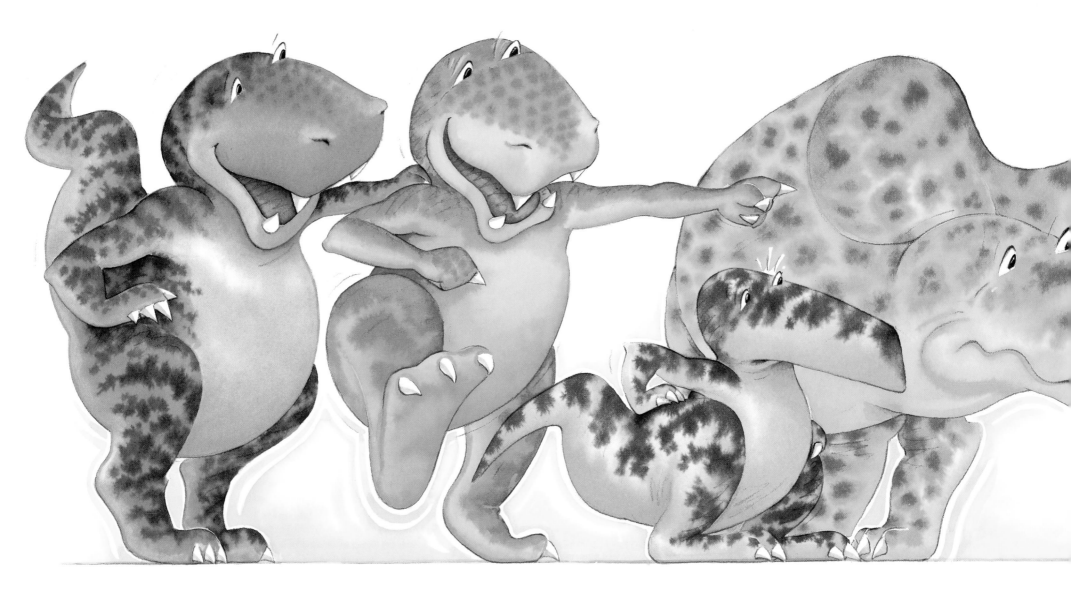

but one got tangled up,

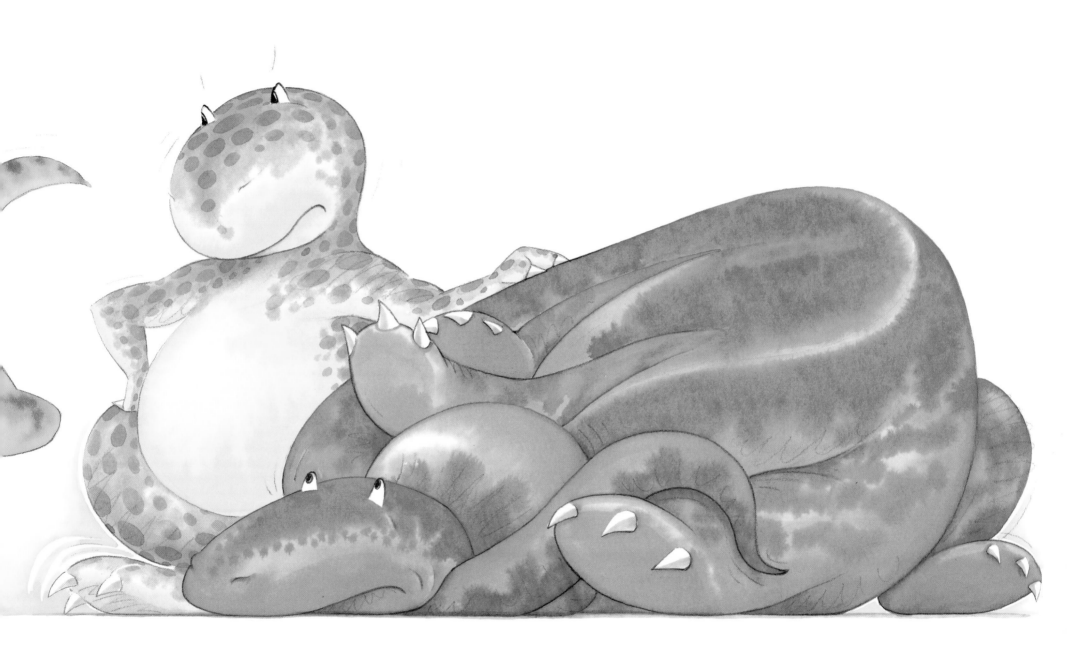

so then there were...

5 feisty dinosaurs

stamping on the floor.

"Quiet down!" cried someone's mom,

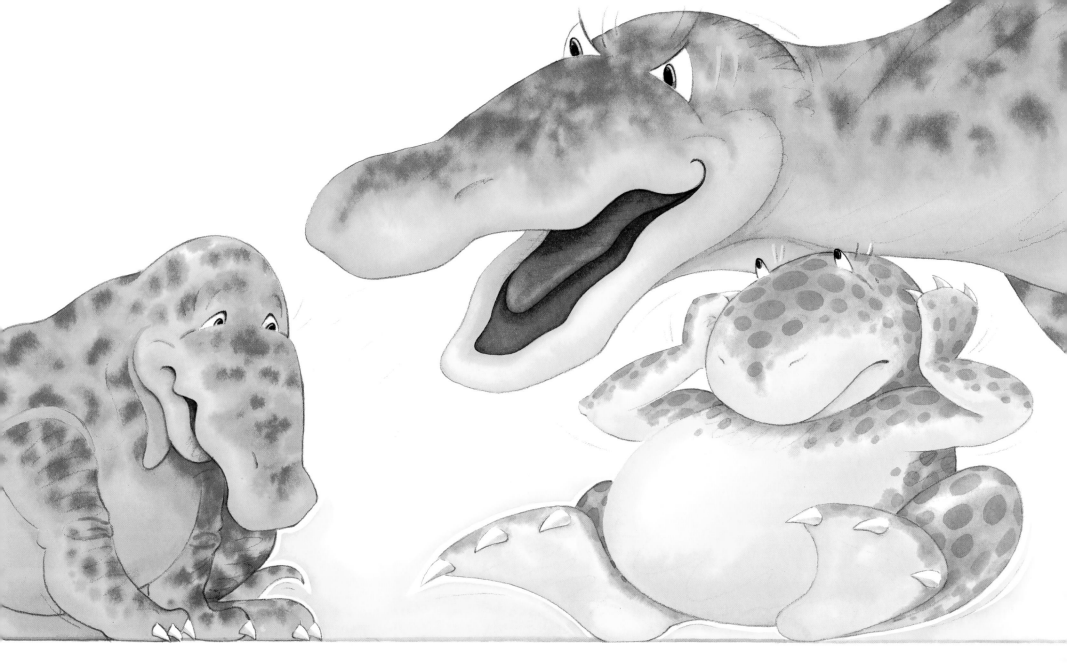

and then there were...

4 fearless dinosaurs

swinging from a tree

but one got stuck

—so then there were...

3 thundering dinosaurs

who flapped and almost flew.

One took off!

So then there were...

2 testy dinosaurs,

tired of all the fun;

one got taken home,

so then there was...

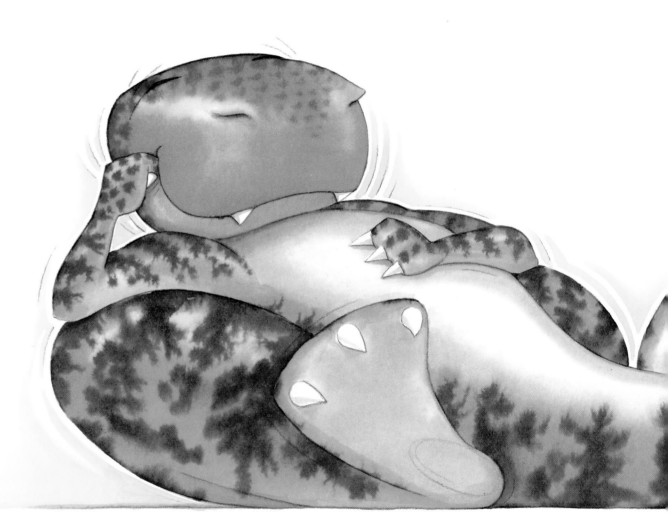

 weary dinosaur

who soon began to snore.

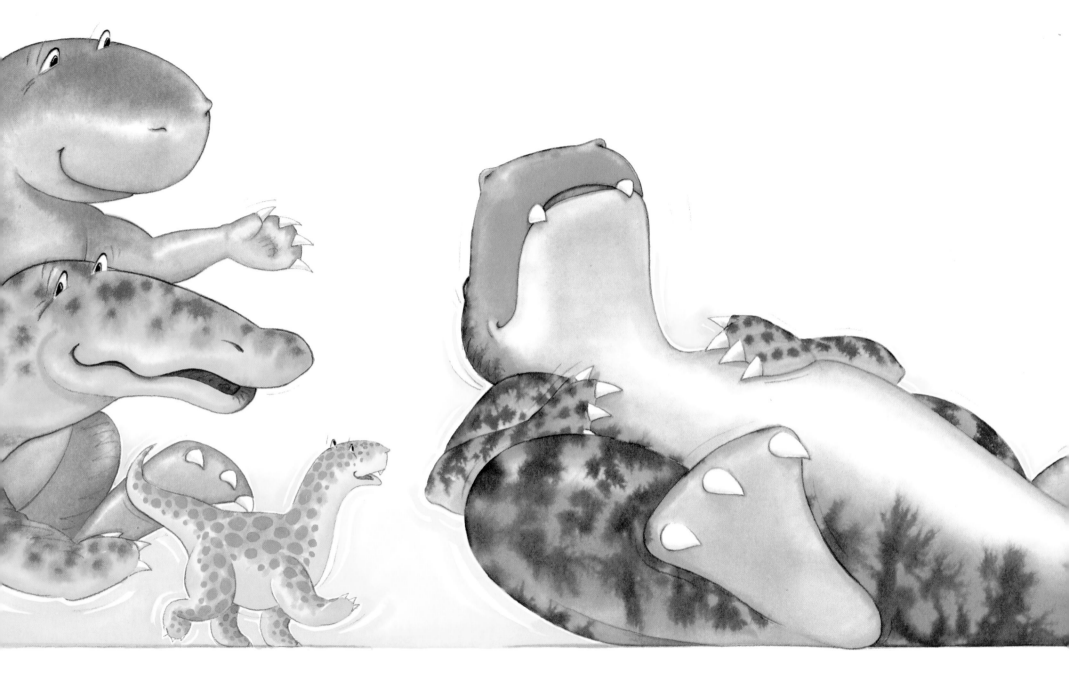

His friends sneaked up behind him

and suddenly yelled...

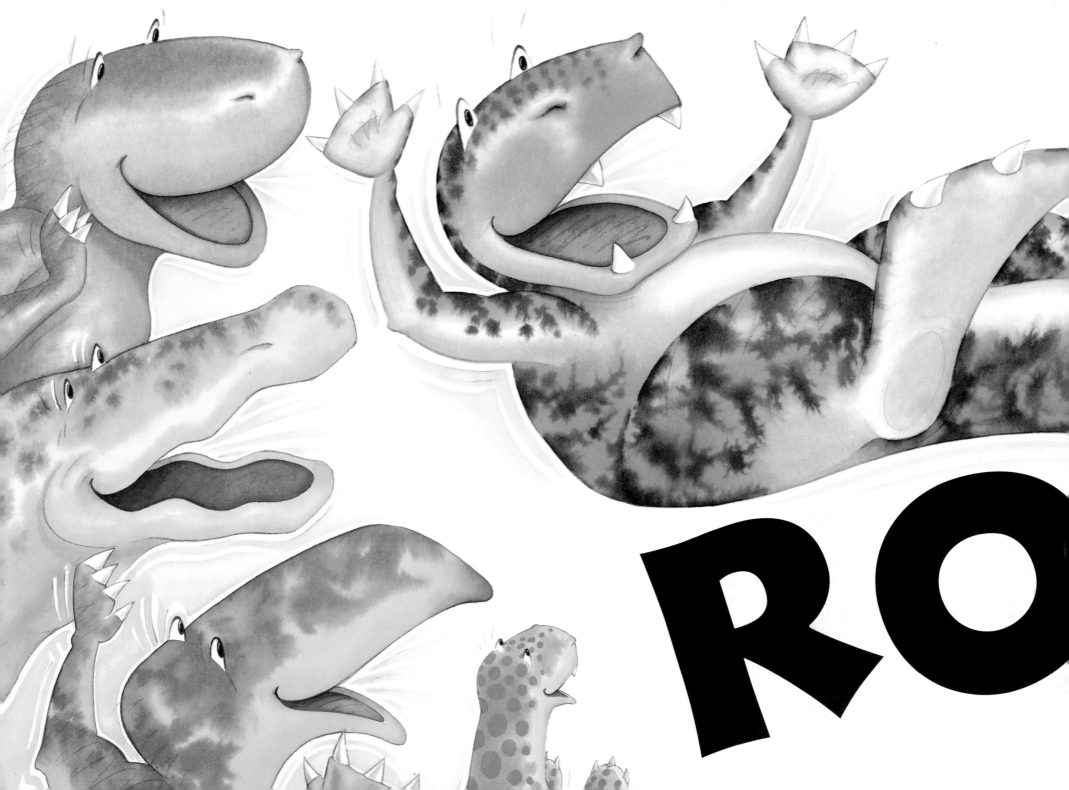

CIP Data is available.
First published in the United States 1997
by Dutton Children's Books,
a member of Penguin Putnam Inc.
375 Hudson Street, New York, New York 10014
Originally published in Great Britain 1997 by
Ragged Bears Limited, Hampshire, England
Typography by Richard Amari
Printed in Singapore
First American Edition   10 9 8 7 6 5 4 3
ISBN 0-525-45905-7